For all you readers who welcomed Mercy into your hearts

K. D.

For Sylvie to read to Oliver

C. V.

Text copyright © 2019 by Kate DiCamillo
Illustrations copyright © 2019 by Chris Van Dusen

First edition 2019

Library of Congress Catalog Card Number 2018961163
ISBN 978-0-7636-7753-4

18 19 20 21 22 23 CCP 10 9 8 7 6 5 4 3 2 1

Printed in Shenzhen, Guangdong, China

This book was typeset in Mrs. Eaves.
The illustrations were done in gouache.

Candlewick Press
99 Dover Street
Somerville, Massachusetts 02144

visit us at www.candlewick.com

A Piglet Named Mercy

Kate DiCamillo

illustrated by

Chris Van Dusen

CANDLEWICK PRESS

Mr. Watson and Mrs. Watson lived in a house on Deckawoo Drive.

Deckawoo Drive was an ordinary street in an ordinary town.

And Mr. and Mrs. Watson were ordinary people who did ordinary things in ordinary ways.

One day, Mrs. Watson said to Mr. Watson,
"I wonder if we aren't just the tiniest bit
   too predictable."

"Predictable? Us?" said Mr. Watson.
"Surely not."

"It's just that sometimes, I wish something
   different would happen," said Mrs. Watson.

"Things are just fine as they are,"
   said Mr. Watson.

But then something different *did* happen.

Someone very small and not at all ordinary found
her way to the Watsons' house on Deckawoo Drive.

Mr. Watson made the discovery when he
opened the door for the morning paper.
"Mrs. Watson!" he called. "Come see!"

"Oh, the little dear," said Mrs. Watson.

"Oink," said the piglet.

"I think she's hungry," said Mr. Watson.

"Is that a pig?" said Eugenia Lincoln.
Eugenia Lincoln lived next door, and she
did not approve of surprises. Or pigs.

"It is!" said Mrs. Watson. "Can you believe our luck?"

"Don't be ridiculous," said Eugenia Lincoln.
"A pig is not lucky at all."

"Do you think perhaps the piglet would like a bottle of warm milk?" said Baby Lincoln. Baby was Eugenia's younger sister, and she was fond of surprises. And piglets.

Mr. Watson scratched his head. "A bottle of milk? I don't know. . . . This is all so unpredictable."

"Leave it to me," said Baby Lincoln.

"Oink!" said the piglet again.

Mrs. Watson picked up the piglet and took her inside. She wrapped her in a blanket. "Have you ever seen anyone so darling?" she said.

"Never," said Mr. Watson.

"Here is the warm milk," said Baby Lincoln.
"I have it right here."

Eugenia said, "This is absurd."

The piglet did not think it was absurd
at all. She drank the entire bottle.

And then she burped.

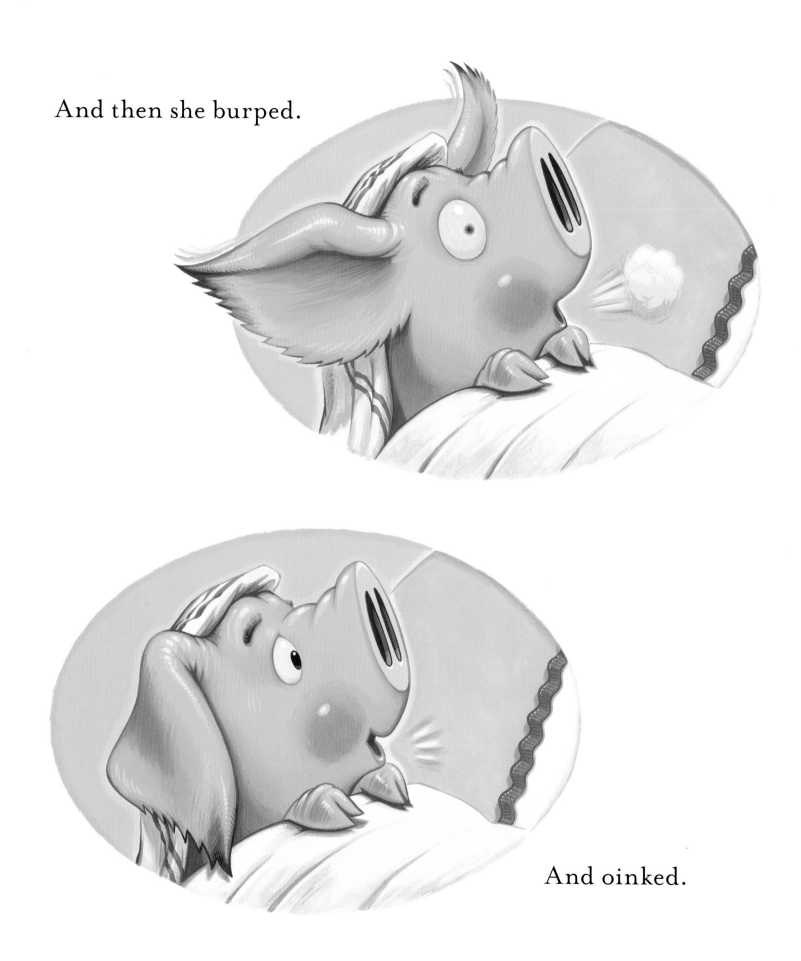

And oinked.

And went looking for more.

"Oh, my goodness," said Mr. Watson.

"Watch out!" said Eugenia.

"She seems to like toast very much!" said Baby.

"Oh, the darling, darling thing," said Mrs. Watson.

"Mr. Watson," said Mrs. Watson, "perhaps you would like to hold her for a bit?"

"Certainly," said Mr. Watson.

He took the piglet in his arms.

He rocked her.

He hummed.

"How extraordinary," said Mr. Watson. "She is a porcine wonder."

"This piglet is a wish come true,"
  said Mrs. Watson.

"What a mercy she is," said Baby.

"There you go," said Mr. Watson.
"We will call her Mercy."

"She is not a mercy," said Eugenia.
"She is a pig."

"Oink, oink," said the piglet.

"You cannot name a pig Mercy!"
  shouted Eugenia.

But they did name her Mercy.

She was entirely unpredictable.

She was not at all ordinary.

And she was very, very loved.